Pippi to the Rescue

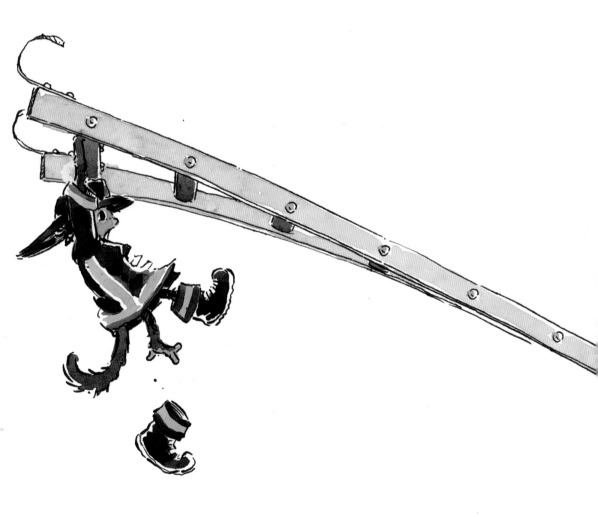

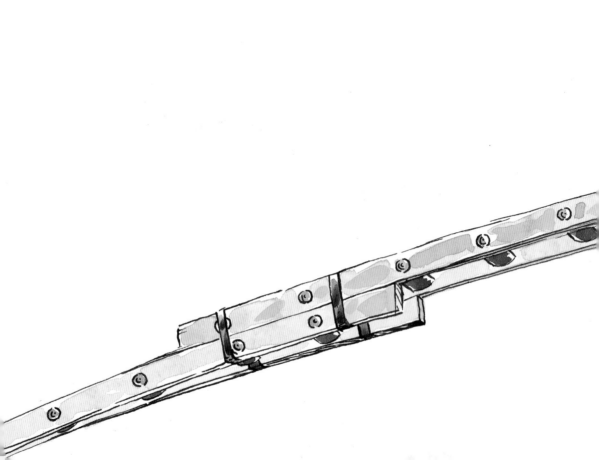

Pippi to the Rescue

by Astrid Lindgren
pictures by Michael Chesworth

VIKING

Way out at the end of a tiny little town was an old overgrown garden, and in the garden was an old house, and in the house lived Pippi Longstocking. She was nine years old, and she lived there all alone. She had no mother and no father, and that was of course very nice because there was no one to tell her to go to bed just when she was having the most fun, and no one who could make her take cod liver oil when she much preferred caramel candy.

Once upon a time Pippi had had a father of whom she was extremely fond. He was a sea captain who sailed on the great ocean, and Pippi had sailed with him in his ship until one day her father was blown overboard in a storm and disappeared. But Pippi was absolutely certain he would come back.

Her father had bought the old house in the garden many years ago. While Pippi was waiting for him to come back she went straight home to live at Villa Villekulla. That was the name of the house.

Two things Pippi took with her from the ship: a little monkey whose name was Mr. Nilsson—he was a present from her father—and a big suitcase full of gold pieces. Pippi also had a horse of her own that she had bought with one of her many gold pieces the day she came home to Villa Villekulla.

Beside Villa Villekulla was another garden and another house. In that house lived a father and mother and two charming children, Tommy and Annika, who often wished for a playmate. And when Pippi Longstocking moved next door, they got the best playmate any child could wish for. This is the story of one of Pippi's adventures. . . .

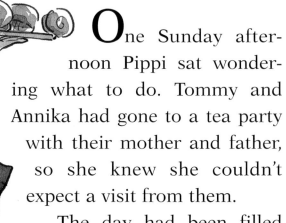

One Sunday after-
noon Pippi sat wonder-
ing what to do. Tommy and
Annika had gone to a tea party
with their mother and father,
so she knew she couldn't
expect a visit from them.

The day had been filled
with pleasant tasks. She had
got up early and served
Mr. Nilsson fruit juice

and buns in bed. He looked
so cute sitting there in
his striped night-
shirt, holding the
glass in both hands.
Then she had fed and
groomed the horse and
told him a long story of
her adventures at sea. Next
she had gone into the par-
lor and painted a large picture on the wallpaper. The
picture represented a

fat lady in a red dress and a black hat. In one hand she held a yellow flower and in the other a dead rat. Pippi thought it a very beautiful picture; it dressed up the whole room. Then she had sat down in front of her chest and looked at all her birds' eggs and shells, and thought about the wonderful places where she and her father had collected them, and about all the pleasant little shops all over the world where they had bought the beautiful things that were now in the drawers of her chest. Then she had tried to teach Mr. Nilsson to dance the schottische, but he didn't want to learn. For a while she had thought of trying to teach the horse, but instead she had crept down into the woodbox and pulled the cover down. She had pretended she was a

sardine in a sardine box, and it was a shame
Tommy and Annika weren't there so they could have
been sardines too.

Now it had begun to grow dark. She pressed her
little pug nose against the windowpane and looked
out into the autumn dusk. She remembered that she
hadn't been riding for a couple of days and decided
to go at once. That would be a nice ending to a pleasant Sunday.

Accordingly she put on her big hat, fetched Mr.
Nilsson from a corner where he sat playing marbles,

saddled the horse, and lifted him down from the porch. And off they went, Mr. Nilsson on Pippi and Pippi on the horse.

It was quite cold and the roads were frozen, so there was a good crunchy sound as they rode along. Mr. Nilsson sat on Pippi's shoulder and tried to catch hold of some of the branches of the trees as they went by, but Pippi rode so fast that it was no use. Instead, the branches kept boxing him in the ears, and he had a hard time keeping his straw hat on his head.

Pippi rode through the little town, and people pressed anxiously up against the walls when she came storming by.

The town had a market square, of course. There were several charming old one-story buildings and a little yellow-painted town hall. And there was also an ugly wretch of a building, newly built and three stories high. It was called "The Skyscraper" because it was taller than any of the other houses in town.

On a Sunday afternoon the little town was always

quiet and peaceful, but suddenly the quiet was bro-
ken by loud cries. "The Skyscraper's burning! Fire!
Fire!"

People came running excitedly from all direc-
tions. The fire engine came clanging down the street,
and the little children who usually thought fire

engines were such fun now cried from fright because they were sure their own houses would catch fire too. The police had to hold back the crowds of

people gathering in the square so that the fire engine could get through. The flames came leaping out of the windows of the Skyscraper, and smoke and sparks enveloped the firemen who were courageously trying to put out the fire. The fire had started on the first floor but was quickly spreading to the upper stories.

Suddenly the crowd saw a sight that made them gasp with horror. At the top of the house was a window, and in the window, which a little child's hand had just opened, stood two little boys calling for help. "We can't get out because somebody has built a fire on the stairs," cried the older boy.

He was five and his brother a year younger. Their mother had gone out on an errand, and there they stood, all alone. Many of the people in the square began to cry, and the fire chief looked worried. There was, of course, a ladder on the fire truck, but it wouldn't reach anywhere near to the little boys. To get into the house to save the children was impossible. A wave of despair swept over the crowd in the square when they realized there was no way to help the children. And the poor little things just stood up there and cried. It wouldn't be long now before the fire reached the attic.

In the midst of the crowd in the square sat Pippi on her horse. She looked with great interest at the fire engine and wondered if she should buy one like it. She liked it because it was red and because it made such a fearful noise as it went through the streets. Then she looked at the fire and she thought it was fun when a few sparks fell on her.

Presently she noticed the little boys up in the attic. To her astonishment they looked as if they weren't enjoying the fire at all. That was more than she could understand, and at last she had to ask the crowd around her, "Why are the children crying?"

First she got only sobs in answer, but finally a stout gentleman said, "Well, what do you think? Don't you suppose you'd cry yourself if you were up there and couldn't get down?"

"I never cry," said Pippi. "But if they want to get down, why doesn't somebody help them?"

"Because it isn't possible, of course," said the stout gentleman.

Pippi thought for a while. Then she asked, "Can anybody bring me a long rope?"

"What good would that do?" asked the stout gentleman. "The children are too small to get down the rope, and, for that matter, how would you ever get the rope up to them?"

"Oh, I've been around a bit," said Pippi calmly. "I want a rope."

There was not a single person who thought it would do any good, but somehow or other Pippi got her rope.

Not far from the Sky-scraper grew a tall tree. The top of it was almost level with the attic window, but between the tree and the window was a distance of almost three yards. And the trunk of the tree was smooth and had no branches for climbing on. Even Pippi wouldn't be able to climb it.

The fire burned. The children in the window screamed. The people in the square cried.

Pippi jumped off the horse and went up to the tree. Then she took the rope and tied it tightly to Mr. Nilsson's tail.

"Now you be Pippi's good boy," she said. She put him on the tree trunk and gave him a little push. He understood perfectly what he was supposed to do. And he climbed obediently up the tree

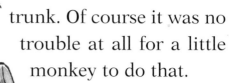

trunk. Of course it was no trouble at all for a little monkey to do that.

The people in the square held their breath and watched Mr. Nilsson. Soon he had reached the top of the tree. There he sat on a branch and looked down at Pippi. She beckoned to him to come down again. He did so at once, climbing down on the other side of the branch, so that when he reached the ground the rope was looped over the branch and hung down double with both ends on the ground.

"Good for you, Mr. Nilsson," said Pippi. "You're so smart you can be a professor any time you wish." She untied the knot that had fastened the rope to Mr. Nilsson's tail.

Nearby, a house was being repaired, and Pippi ran over and got a long board. She took the board in one hand, ran to the tree, grasped the rope in her free hand, and braced her feet against the trunk of the tree. Quickly and nimbly she climbed up the trunk, and the people stopped crying in astonishment. When she reached the top of the tree she placed the board over a stout branch and then carefully pushed it over to the windowsill. And there lay the board like a bridge between the top of the tree and the window.

The people down in the square stood absolutely silent. They were so tense they couldn't say a word. Pippi stepped out on the board. She smiled pleasantly at the two boys in the window. "Why do you look so sad?" she asked. "Have you got a stomach-ache?"

She ran across the board and hopped in at the window. "My, it seems warm in here," she said. "You don't need to make any more fire in here today, that I can guarantee. And at the most four sticks in the stove tomorrow, I should think."

Then she took one boy under each arm and stepped out on the board again.

"Now you're really going to have some fun," she said. "It's almost like walking the tightrope."

When she got to the middle of the board she lifted one leg in the air as if she was on a tightrope. The crowd below gasped, and when a little later Pippi lost one of her shoes several old ladies fainted. However, Pippi reached the tree safely with the little boys. Then the crowd cheered so loudly that the dark night was filled with noise and the sound drowned out the crackling of the fire.

Pippi
hauled up
the rope, fastened one end
securely to a branch and tied
the other around one of the
boys. Then she let
him down slowly and care-
fully into the arms of his
waiting mother, who
was beside herself with
joy when she had him
safe. She held him
close and hugged
him, with tears
in her eyes.

But Pippi
yelled, "Untie the
rope, for goodness' sake! There's

another kid up here, and he can't fly either."

So the people helped to untie the rope and free the little boy. Pippi could tie good knots, she could indeed. She had learned that at sea. She pulled up the rope again, and now it was the second boy's turn to be let down.

Pippi was alone in the tree. She sprang out on the board, and all the people looked at her and wondered what she was going to do. She danced back and forth on the narrow board. She raised and lowered her arms gracefully and sang in a hoarse voice that could barely be heard down in the square:

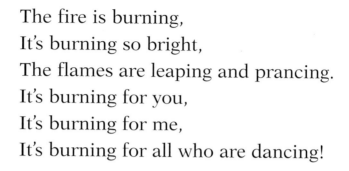

The fire is burning,
It's burning so bright,
The flames are leaping and prancing.
It's burning for you,
It's burning for me,
It's burning for all who are dancing!

As she sang she danced more and more wildly until many people covered their eyes in horror, for they were sure she would fall down and kill herself. Flames came leaping out of the window, and in the firelight people could see Pippi plainly. She raised her arms to the night sky, and while a shower of sparks fell over her she cried loudly, "Such a jolly, jolly fire!"

She took one leap and caught the rope. "Look out!" she cried and came sliding down the rope like greased lightning.

"Three cheers for Pippi Longstocking! Long may she live!" cried the fire chief.

"Hip, hip, hurray! Hip, hip, hurray! Hip, hip, hurray!" cried all the people—three times. But there was one person there who cheered four times.

It was Pippi Longstocking.

The text in this book has been excerpted, with Astrid Lindgren's assistance,
from two chapters in *Pippi Longstocking*.

VIKING
Published by the Penguin Group
Penguin Putnam Books for Young Readers, 345 Hudson Street, New York, New York 10014, U.S.A.

Penguin Books Ltd, Registered Offices: Harmondsworth, Middlesex, England

First published in 2000 by Viking, a division of Penguin Putnam Books for Young Readers.

1 3 5 7 9 10 8 6 4 2

LIBRARY OF CONGRESS CATALOGING-IN-PUBLICATION DATA
Lindgren, Astrid, date–
Pippi to the rescue/by Astrid Lindgren ; pictures by Michael Chesworth.
p. cm. — (A Pippi Longstocking storybook)
Summary: The heroic Pippi Longstocking takes charge and rescues two little boys from a
burning building when no one else can figure out how to save them.
ISBN 0-670-88074-4
[1. Heroes—Fiction. 2. Fires—Fiction. 3. Sweden—Fiction.] I. Chesworth, Michael, ill II. Title.
PZ7.L6585 Pr 2000 [E]—dc21 99-056111

Printed in Hong Kong
Set in New Aster